D0605306

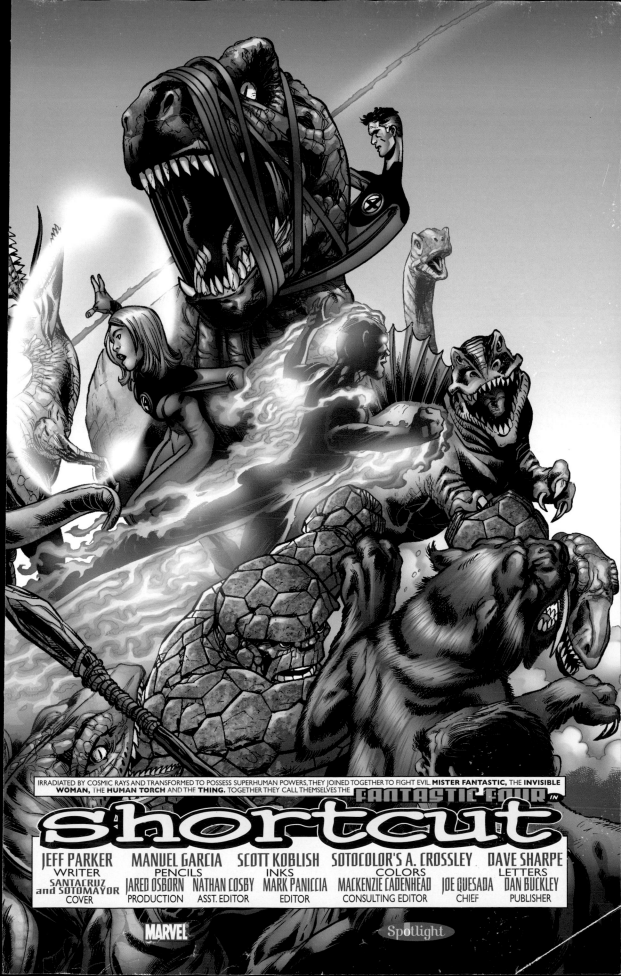

IRRADIATED BY COSMIC RAYS AND TRANSFORMED TO POSSESS SUPERHUMAN POWERS, THEY JOINED TOGETHER TO FIGHT EVIL. **MISTER FANTASTIC**, THE **INVISIBLE WOMAN**, THE **HUMAN TORCH** AND THE **THING**. TOGETHER THEY CALL THEMSELVES THE **FANTASTIC FOUR** IN

shortcut

JEFF PARKER
WRITER

MANUEL GARCIA
PENCILS

SCOTT KOBLISH
INKS

SOTOCOLOR'S A. CROSSLEY
COLORS

DAVE SHARPE
LETTERS

SANTACRUZ
and SOTOMAYOR
COVER

JARED OSBORN
PRODUCTION

NATHAN COSBY
ASST. EDITOR

MARK PANICCIA
EDITOR

MACKENZIE CADENHEAD
CONSULTING EDITOR

JOE QUESADA
CHIEF

DAN BUCKLEY
PUBLISHER

MARVEL

Spotlight

VISIT US AT
www.abdopublishing.com

Spotlight library bound edition © 2007. Spotlight is a division of ABDO Publishing Company, Edina, Minnesota.

Cataloging Data

Parker, Jeff
    Fantastic Four in shortcut / Jeff Parker, writer ; Manuel Garcia, pencils ; Scott Koblish, inks. -- Library bound ed.
        p. cm. -- (Fantastic Four)
    Summary: Irradiated by cosmic rays and transformed to possess superhuman powers, Mr. Fantastic, the Invisible Woman, the Human Torch, and the Thing join together to fight evil.
    "Marvel age"--Cover.
    Revision of the December 2005 issue of Marvel adventures Fantastic Four.
    ISBN-13: 978-1-59961-204-1
    ISBN-10: 1-59961-204-6
    1. Fantastic Four (Fictitious characters)--Comic books, strips, etc.--Fiction. 2. Graphic novels. I. Title. II. Title: Shortcut III. Series.

    741.5dc22

All Spotlight books are reinforced library binding
and manufactured in the United States of America

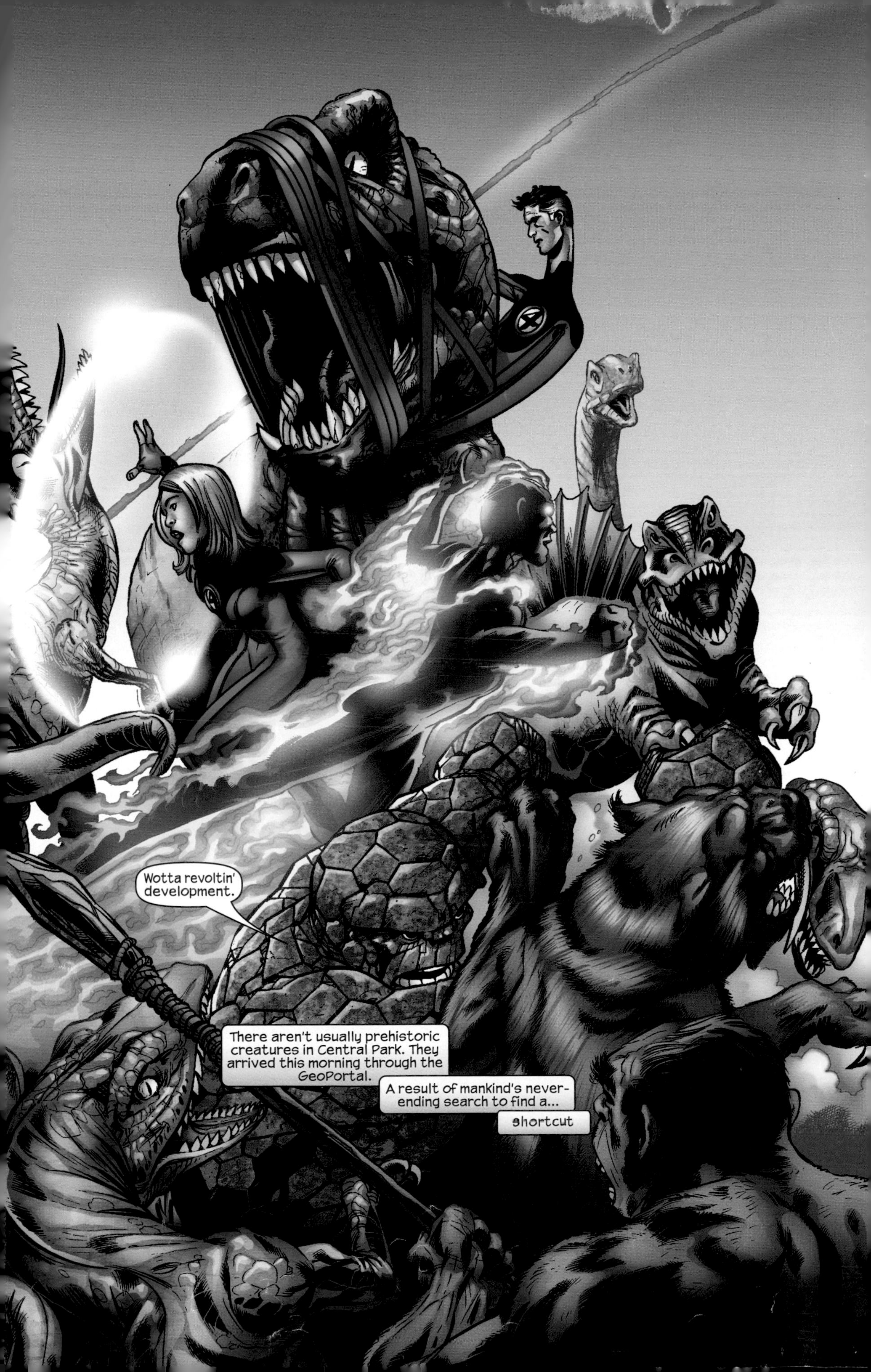
Wotta revoltin' development.
There aren't usually prehistoric creatures in Central Park. They arrived this morning through the GeoPortal.
A result of mankind's never-ending search to find a...
shortcut

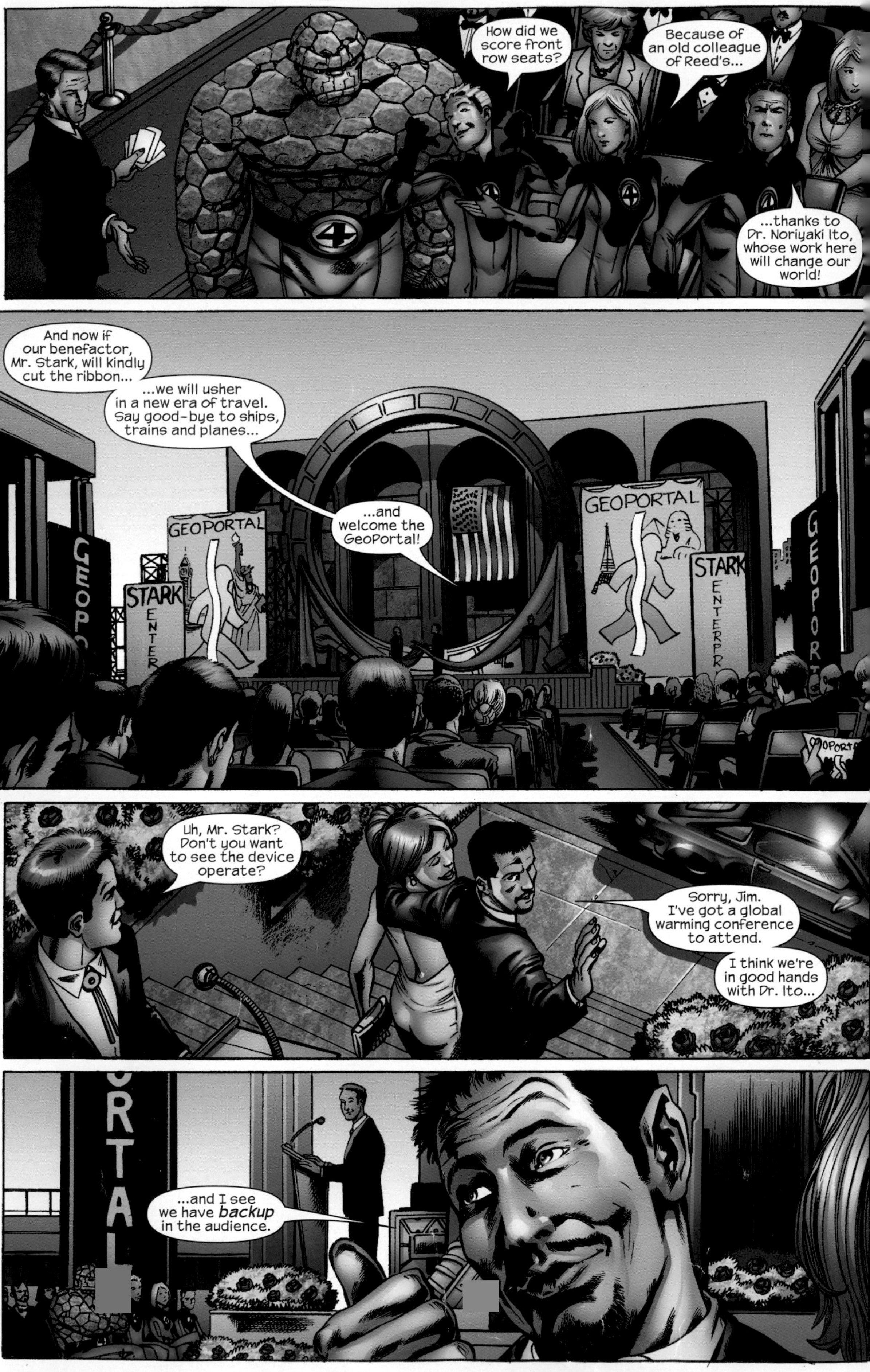
How did we score front row seats?
Because of an old colleague of Reed's...
...thanks to Dr. Noriyaki Ito, whose work here will change our world!
And now if our benefactor, Mr. Stark, will kindly cut the ribbon...
...we will usher in a new era of travel. Say good-bye to ships, trains and planes...
...and welcome the GeoPortal!
GEOPORTAL
STARK
GEOPORTAL
STARK
Uh, Mr. Stark? Don't you want to see the device operate?
Sorry, Jim. I've got a global warming conference to attend.
I think we're in good hands with Dr. Ito...
...and I see we have *backup* in the audience.

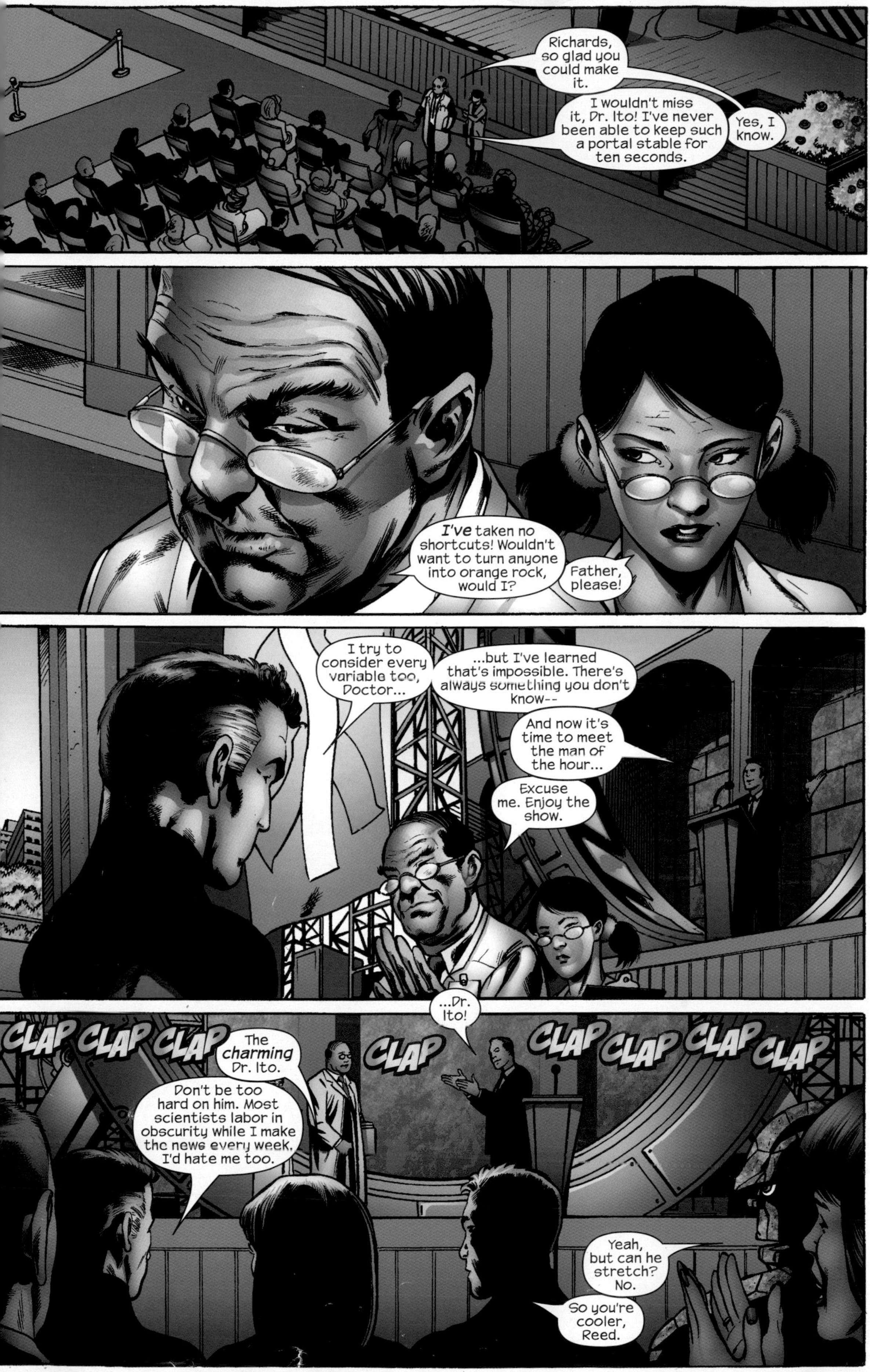
Richards, so glad you could make it.
I wouldn't miss it, Dr. Ito! I've never been able to keep such a portal stable for ten seconds.
Yes, I know.
I've taken no shortcuts! Wouldn't want to turn anyone into orange rock, would I?
Father, please!
I try to consider every variable too, Doctor...
...but I've learned that's impossible. There's always something you don't know--
And now it's time to meet the man of the hour...
Excuse me. Enjoy the show.
...Dr. Ito!
CLAP CLAP CLAP
The *charming* Dr. Ito.
CLAP
CLAP CLAP CLAP CLAP
Don't be too hard on him. Most scientists labor in obscurity while I make the news every week. I'd hate me too.
Yeah, but can he stretch? No.
So you're cooler, Reed.

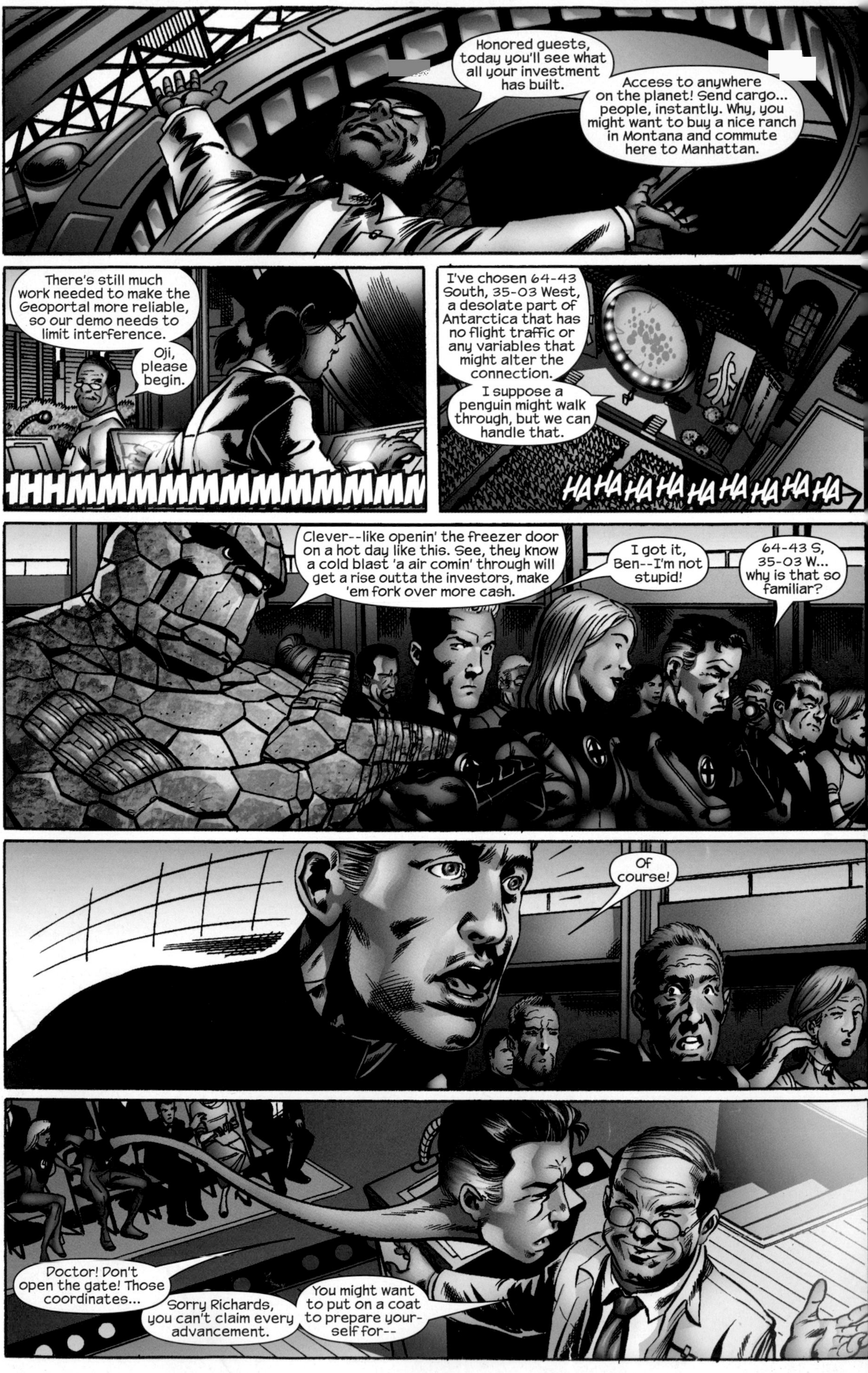
Honored guests, today you'll see what all your investment has built.
Access to anywhere on the planet! Send cargo... people, instantly. Why, you might want to buy a nice ranch in Montana and commute here to Manhattan.
There's still much work needed to make the Geoportal more reliable, so our demo needs to limit interference.
Oji, please begin.
HHMMMMMMMMMMMMMMMMN
I've chosen 64-43 South, 35-03 West, a desolate part of Antarctica that has no flight traffic or any variables that might alter the connection.
I suppose a penguin might walk through, but we can handle that.
HA HA HA HA HA HA HA HA HA
Clever--like openin' the freezer door on a hot day like this. See, they know a cold blast 'a air comin' through will get a rise outta the investors, make 'em fork over more cash.
I got it, Ben--I'm not stupid!
64-43 S, 35-03 W... why is that so familiar?
Of course!
Doctor! Don't open the gate! Those coordinates...
Sorry Richards, you can't claim every advancement.
You might want to put on a coat to prepare your-self for--

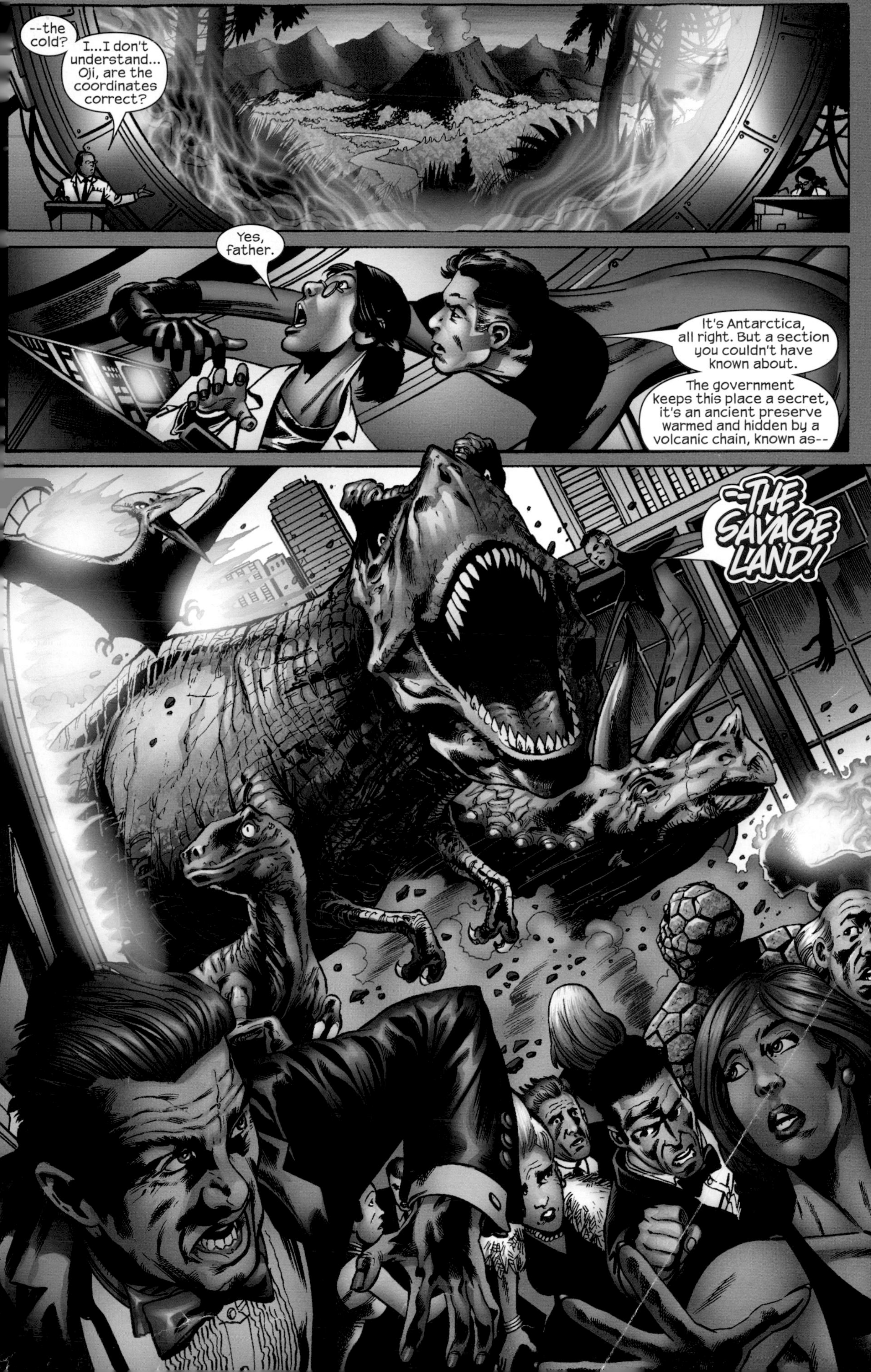
--the cold?
I...I don't understand... Oji, are the coordinates correct?
Yes, father.
It's Antarctica, all right. But a section you couldn't have known about.
The government keeps this place a secret, it's an ancient preserve warmed and hidden by a volcanic chain, known as--
--THE SAVAGE LAND!

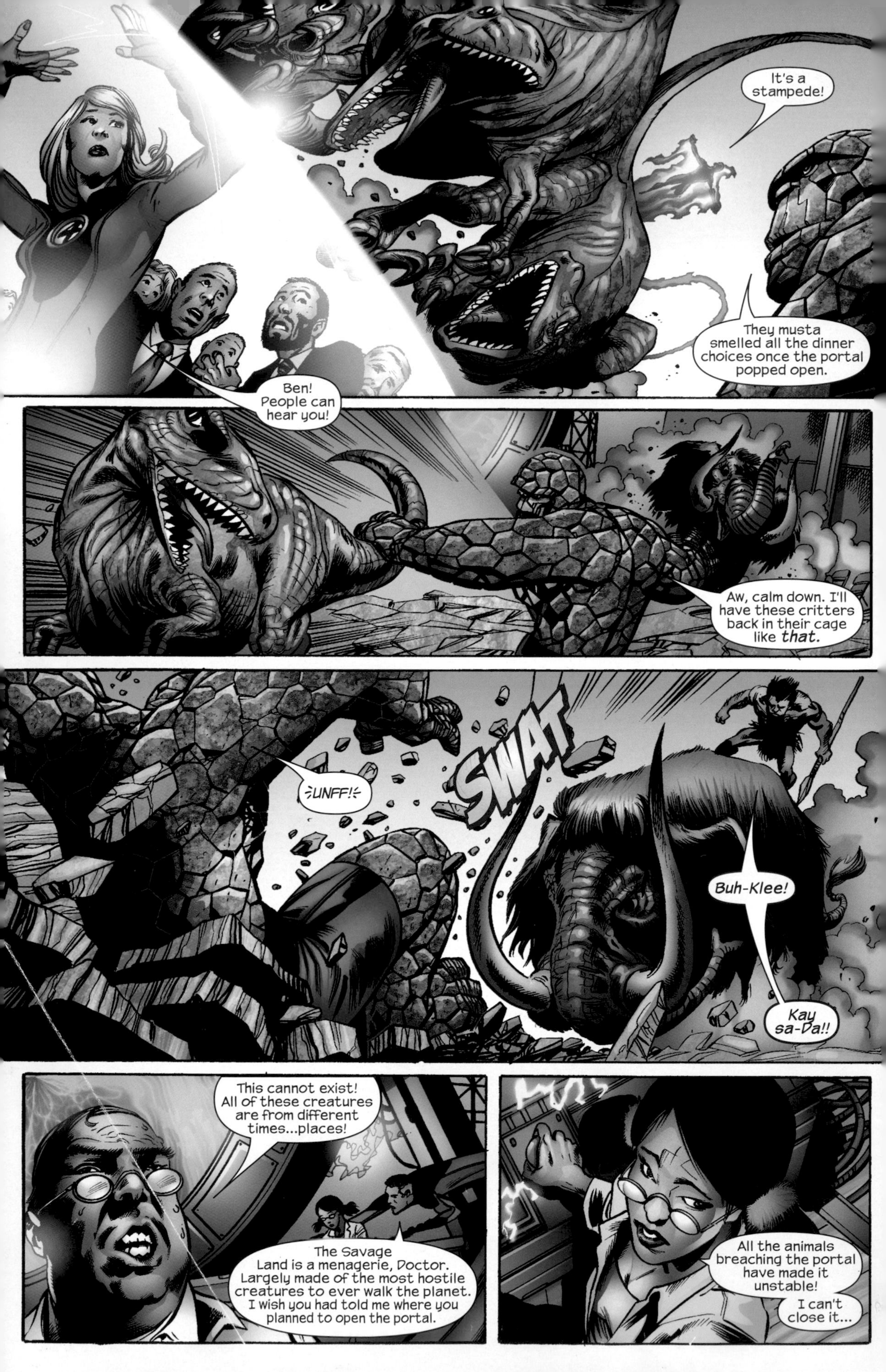
It's a stampede!
They musta smelled all the dinner choices once the portal popped open.
Ben! People can hear you!
Aw, calm down. I'll have these critters back in their cage like *that.*
UNFF!
SWAT
Buh-Klee!
Kay sa-Da!!
This cannot exist! All of these creatures are from different times...places!
The Savage Land is a menagerie, Doctor. Largely made of the most hostile creatures to ever walk the planet. I wish you had told me where you planned to open the portal.
All the animals breaching the portal have made it unstable!
I can't close it...

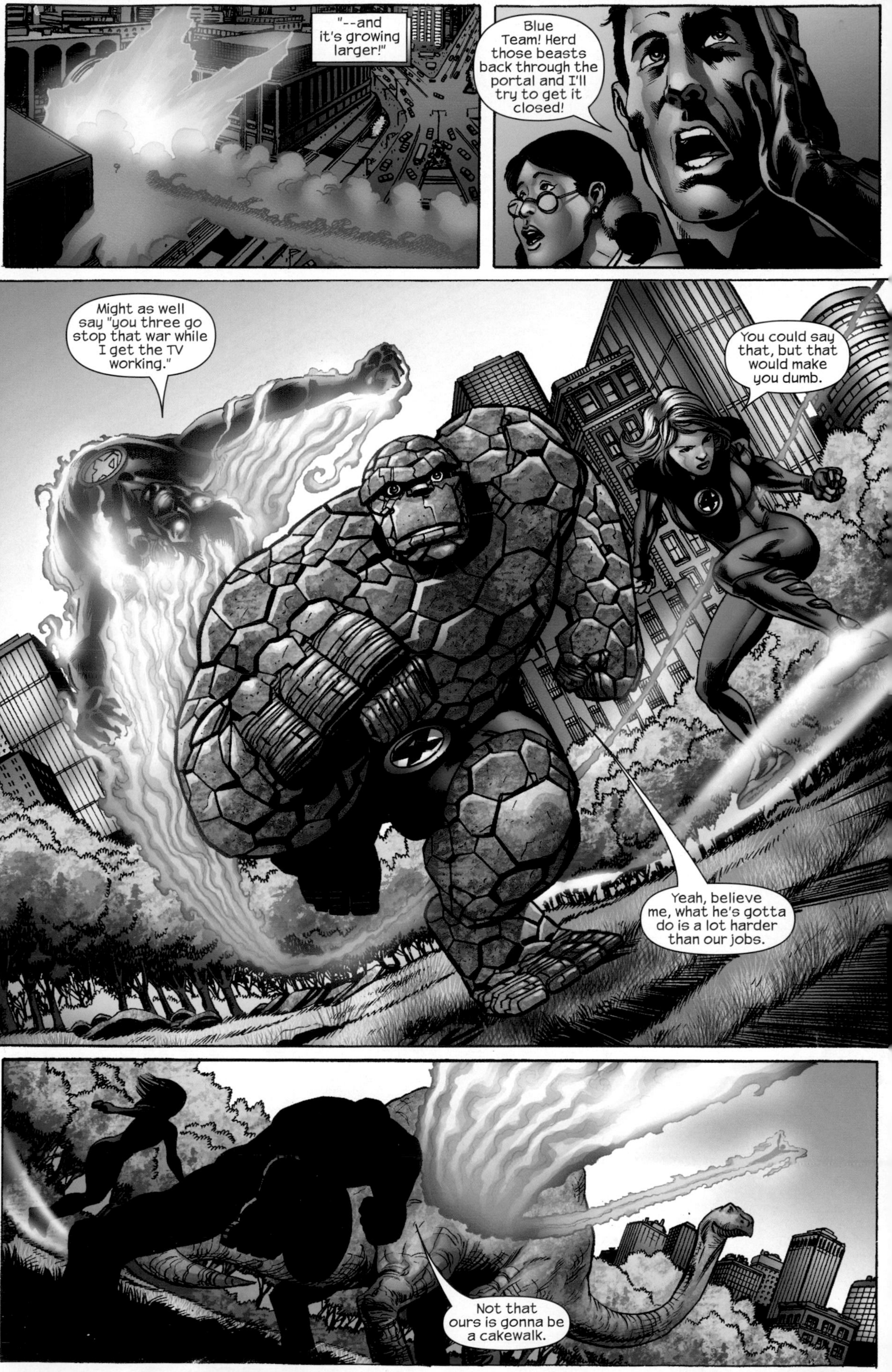

"--and it's growing larger!"
Blue Team! Herd those beasts back through the portal and I'll try to get it closed!
Might as well say "you three go stop that war while I get the TV working."
You could say that, but that would make you dumb.
Yeah, believe me, what he's gotta do is a lot harder than our jobs.
Not that ours is gonna be a cakewalk.

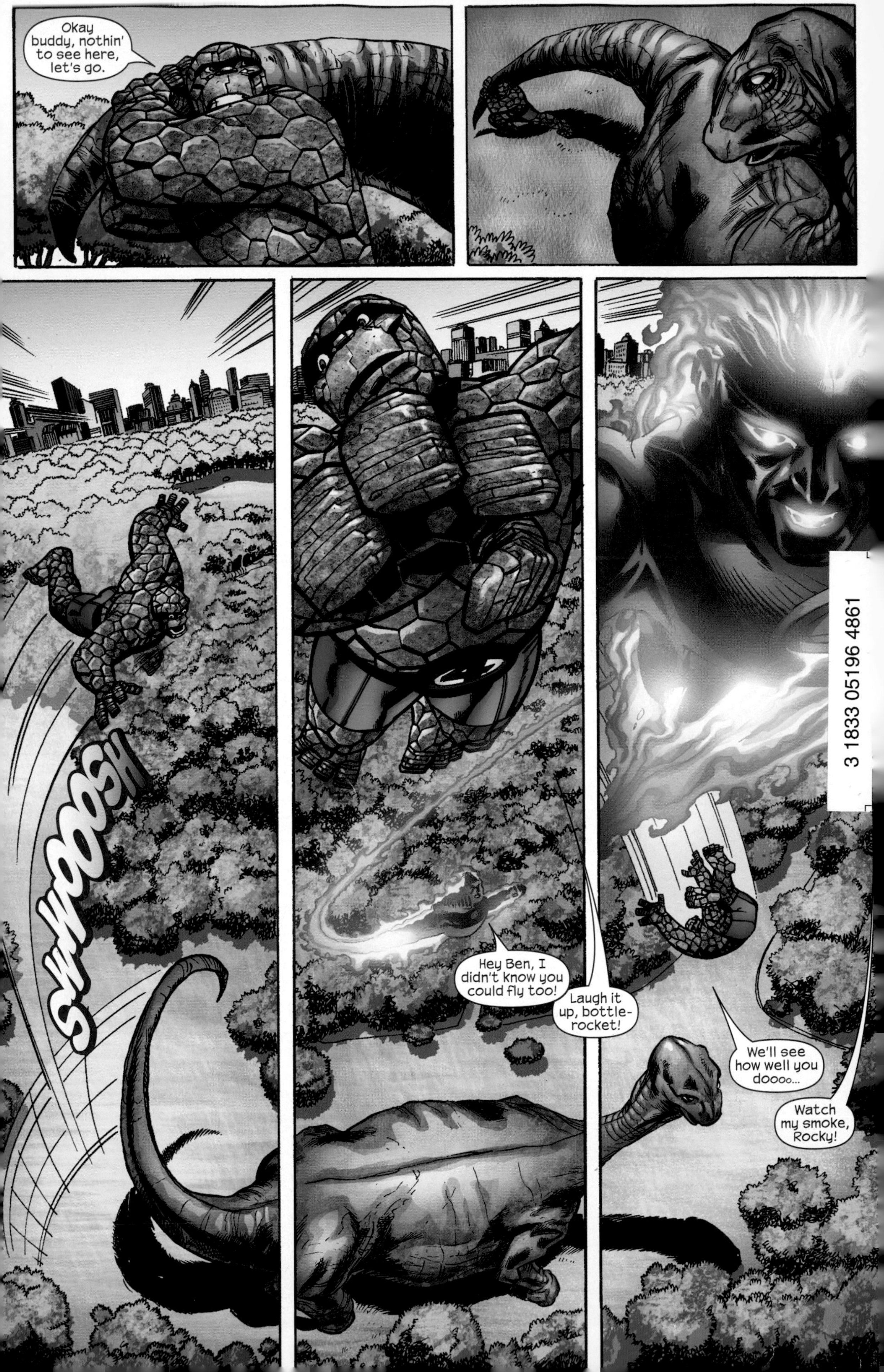
Okay buddy, nothin' to see here, let's go.
SWHOOOSH
Hey Ben, I didn't know you could fly too!
Laugh it up, bottle-rocket!
We'll see how well you doooo...
Watch my smoke, Rocky!

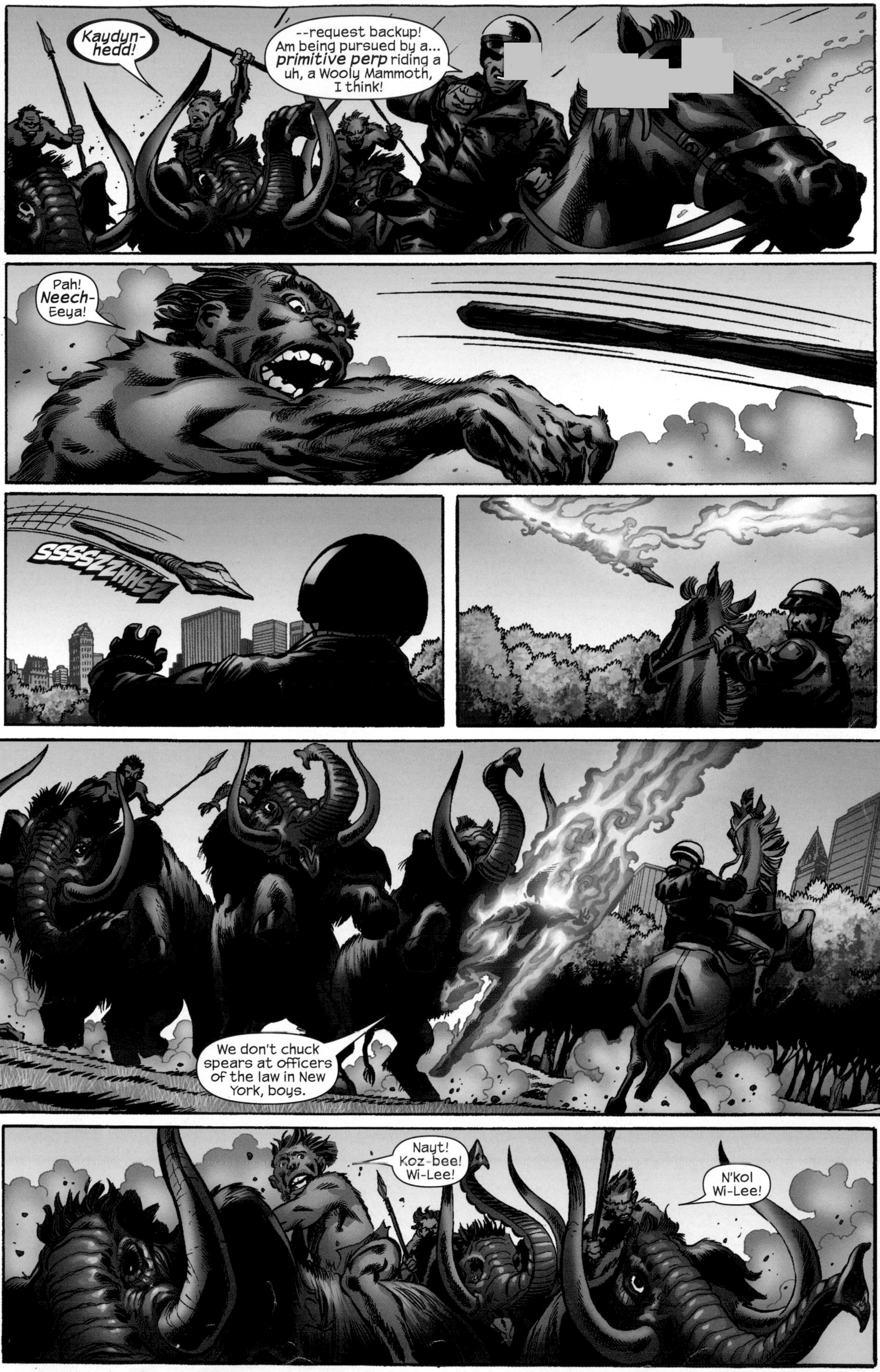
Kaydun-hedd!
--request backup! Am being pursued by a... primitive perp riding a uh, a Wooly Mammoth, I think!
Pah! Neech-Eeya!
SSSSZZHHSZ
We don't chuck spears at officers of the law in New York, boys.
Nayt! Koz-bee! Wi-Lee!
N'Kol Wi-Lee!

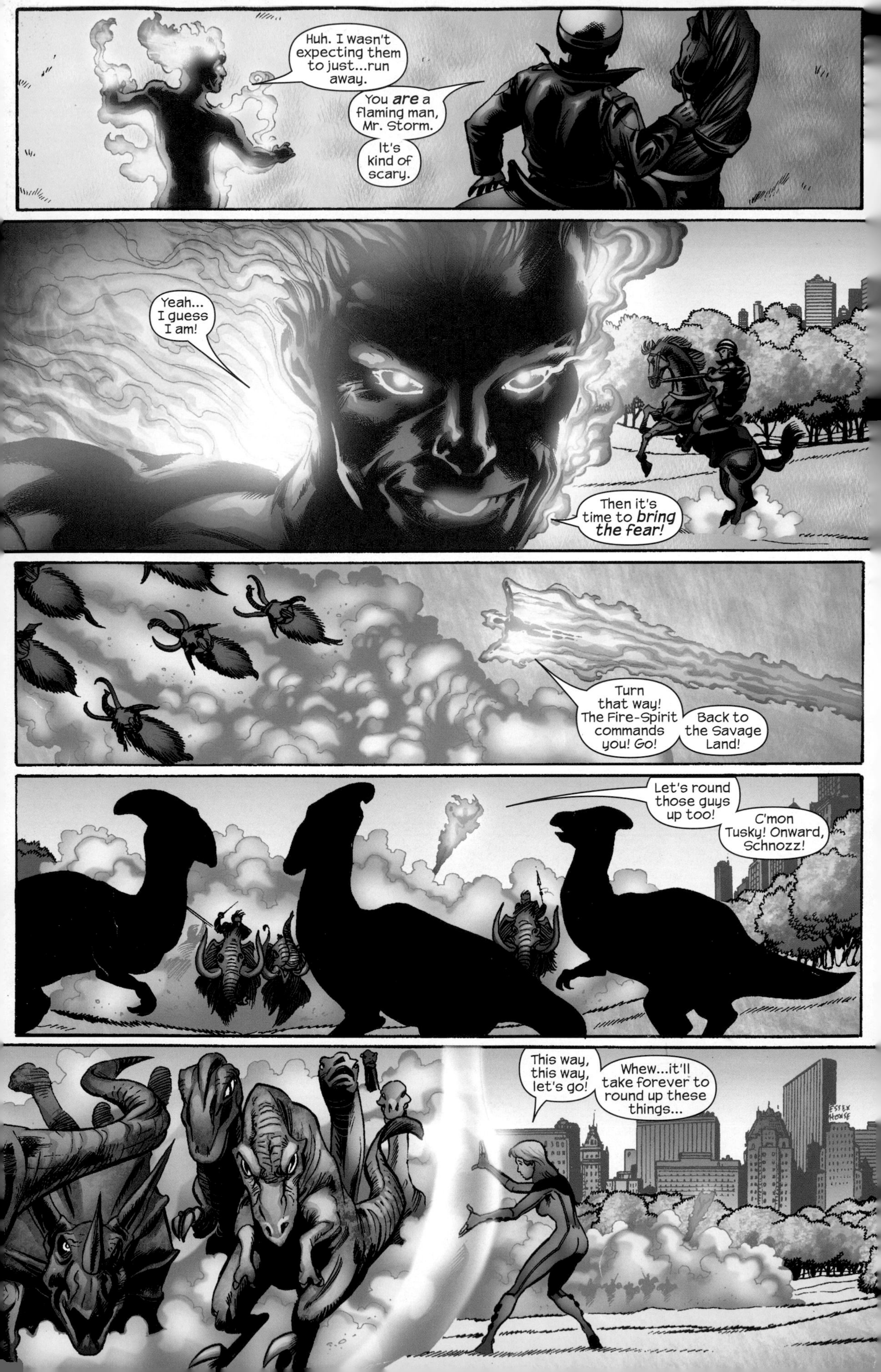

Huh. I wasn't expecting them to just...run away.
You **are** a flaming man, Mr. Storm.
It's kind of scary.
Yeah... I guess I am!
Then it's time to ***bring the fear!***
Turn that way! The Fire-Spirit commands you! Go!
Back to the Savage Land!
Let's round those guys up too!
C'mon Tusky! Onward, Schnozz!
This way, this way, let's go!
Whew...it'll take forever to round up these things...
ESSEX HOUSE

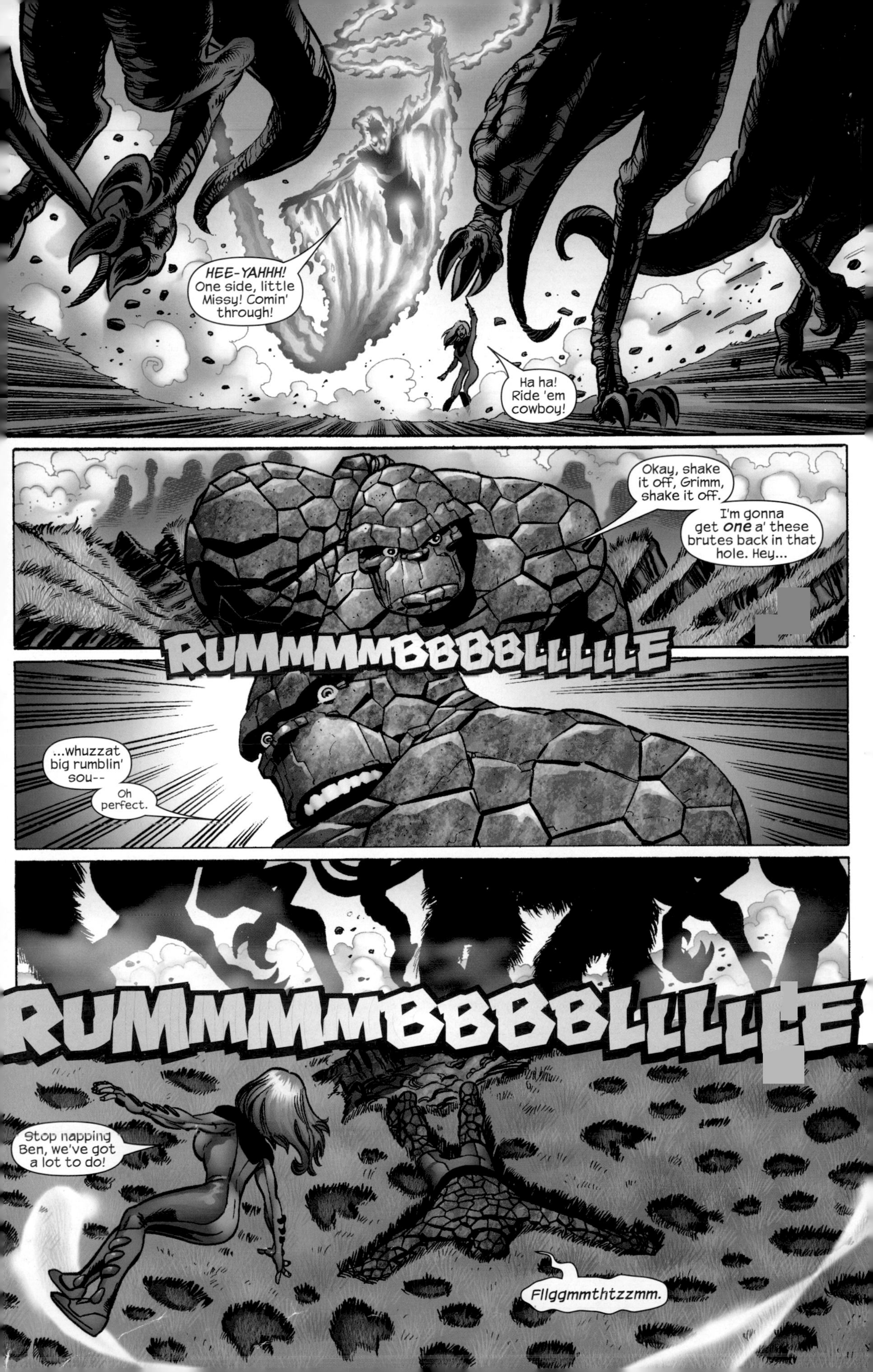
HEE-YAHHH! One side, little Missy! Comin' through!
Ha ha! Ride 'em cowboy!
Okay, shake it off, Grimm, shake it off.
I'm gonna get one a' these brutes back in that hole. Hey...
RUMMMMMBBBBLLLLLE
...whuzzat big rumblin' sou--
Oh perfect.
RUMMMMMMBBBBLLLLLE
Stop napping Ben, we've got a lot to do!
Fllggmmthtzzmm.

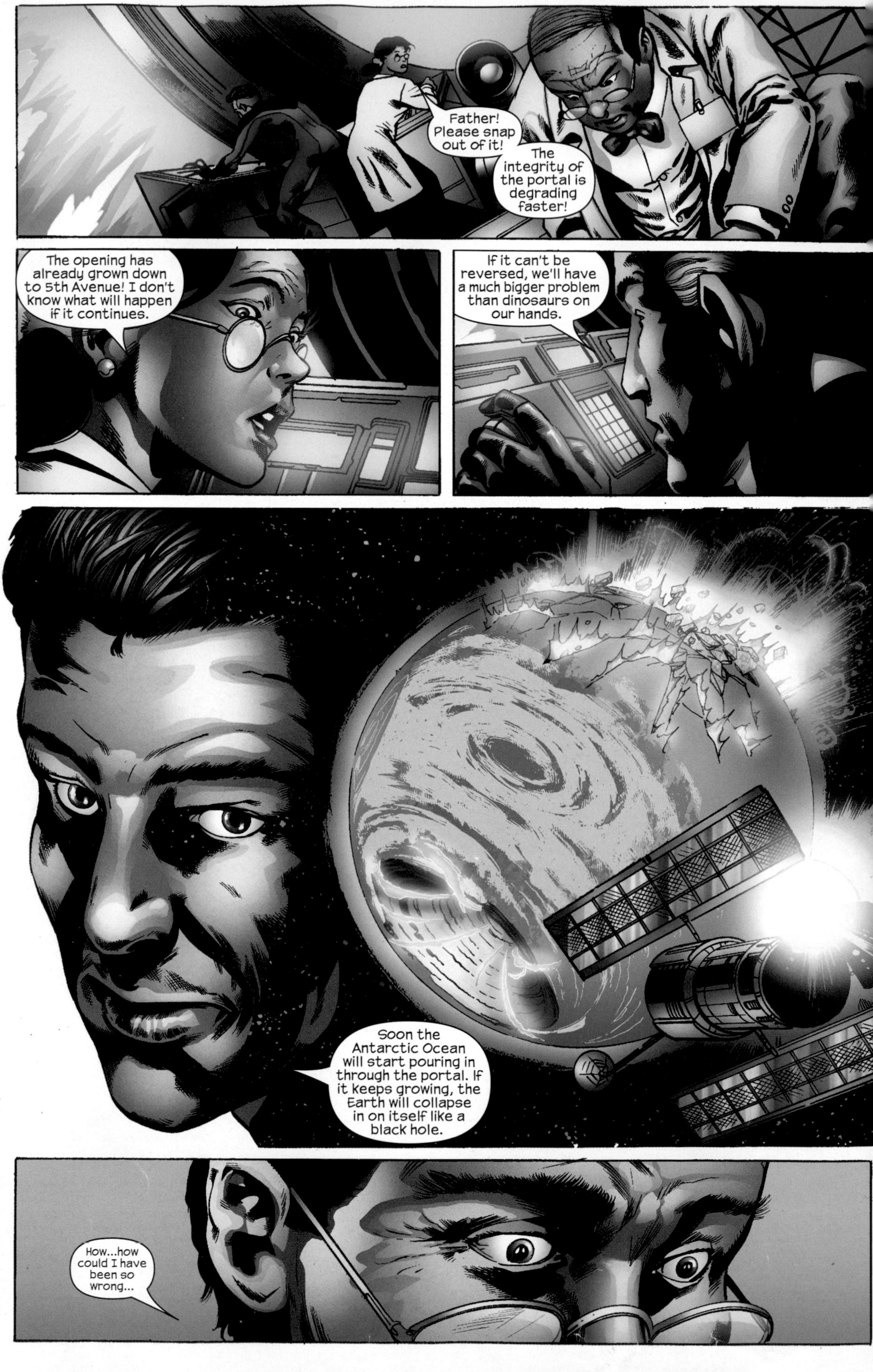
Father! Please snap out of it!
The integrity of the portal is degrading faster!
The opening has already grown down to 5th Avenue! I don't know what will happen if it continues.
If it can't be reversed, we'll have a much bigger problem than dinosaurs on our hands.
Soon the Antarctic Ocean will start pouring in through the portal. If it keeps growing, the Earth will collapse in on itself like a black hole.
How...how could I have been so wrong...

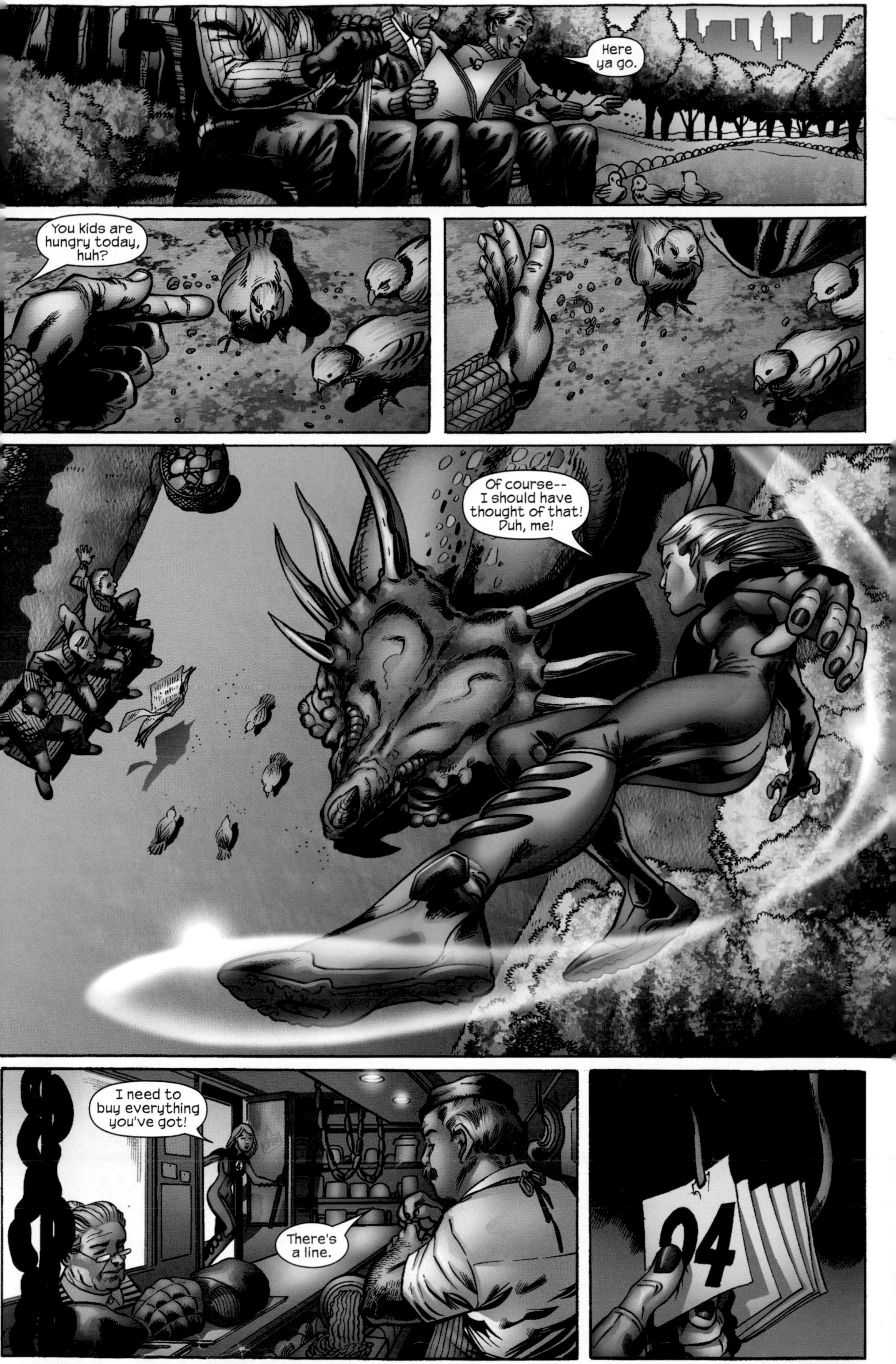
Here ya go.
You kids are hungry today, huh?
Of course-- I should have thought of that! Duh, me!
I need to buy everything you've got!
There's a line.
04

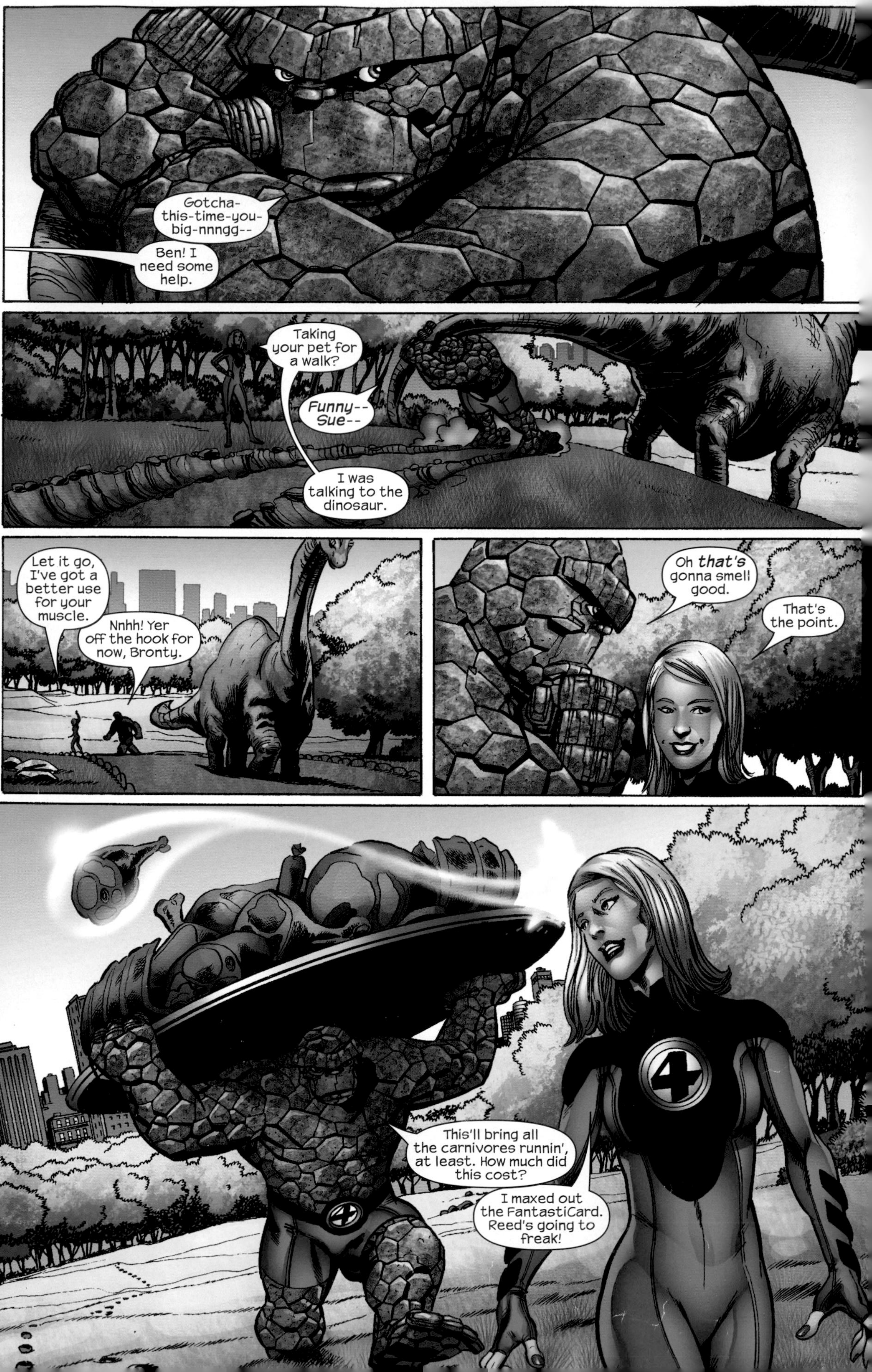
Gotcha-this-time-you-big-nnngg--
Ben! I need some help.
Taking your pet for a walk?
Funny--Sue--
I was talking to the dinosaur.
Let it go, I've got a better use for your muscle.
Nnhh! Yer off the hook for now, Bronty.
Oh that's gonna smell good.
That's the point.
This'll bring all the carnivores runnin', at least. How much did this cost?
I maxed out the FantastiCard. Reed's going to freak!

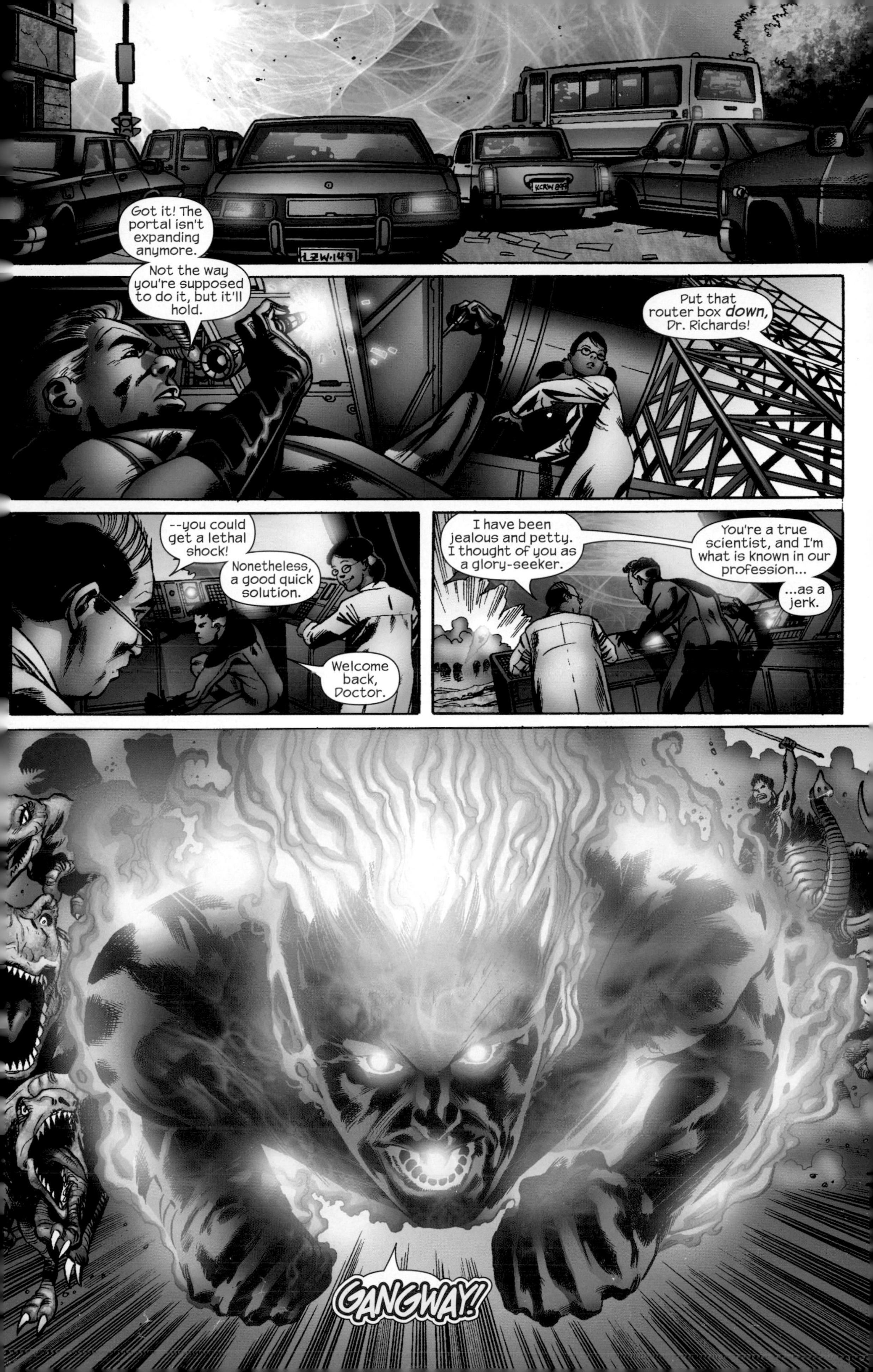

Got it! The portal isn't expanding anymore.
Not the way you're supposed to do it, but it'll hold.
Put that router box *down,* Dr. Richards!
--you could get a lethal shock!
Nonetheless, a good quick solution.
Welcome back, Doctor.
I have been jealous and petty. I thought of you as a glory-seeker.
You're a true scientist, and I'm what is known in our profession...
...as a jerk.
GANGWAY!

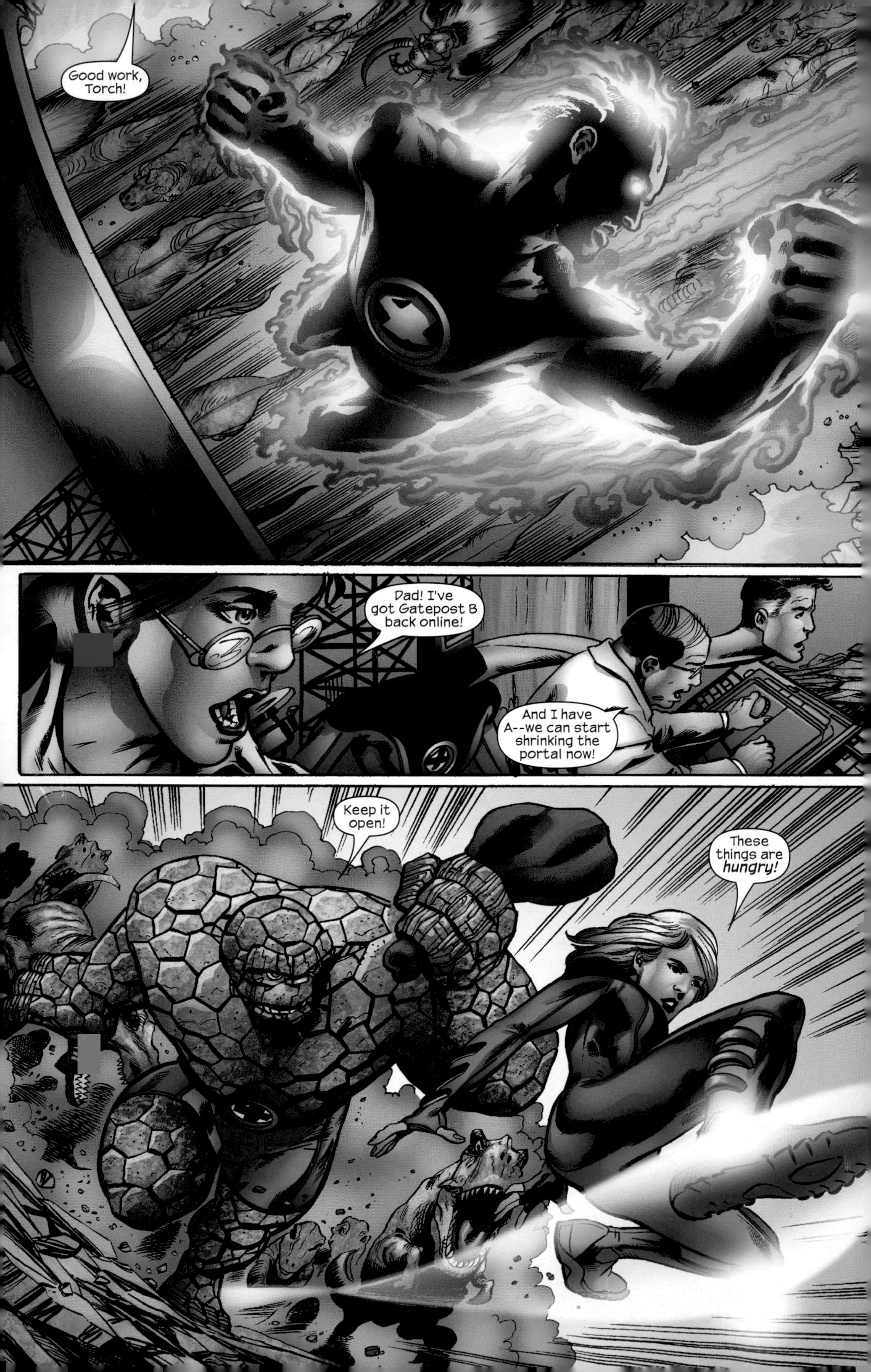
Good work, Torch!
Dad! I've got Gatepost B back online!
And I have A--we can start shrinking the portal now!
Keep it open!
These things are *hungry!*

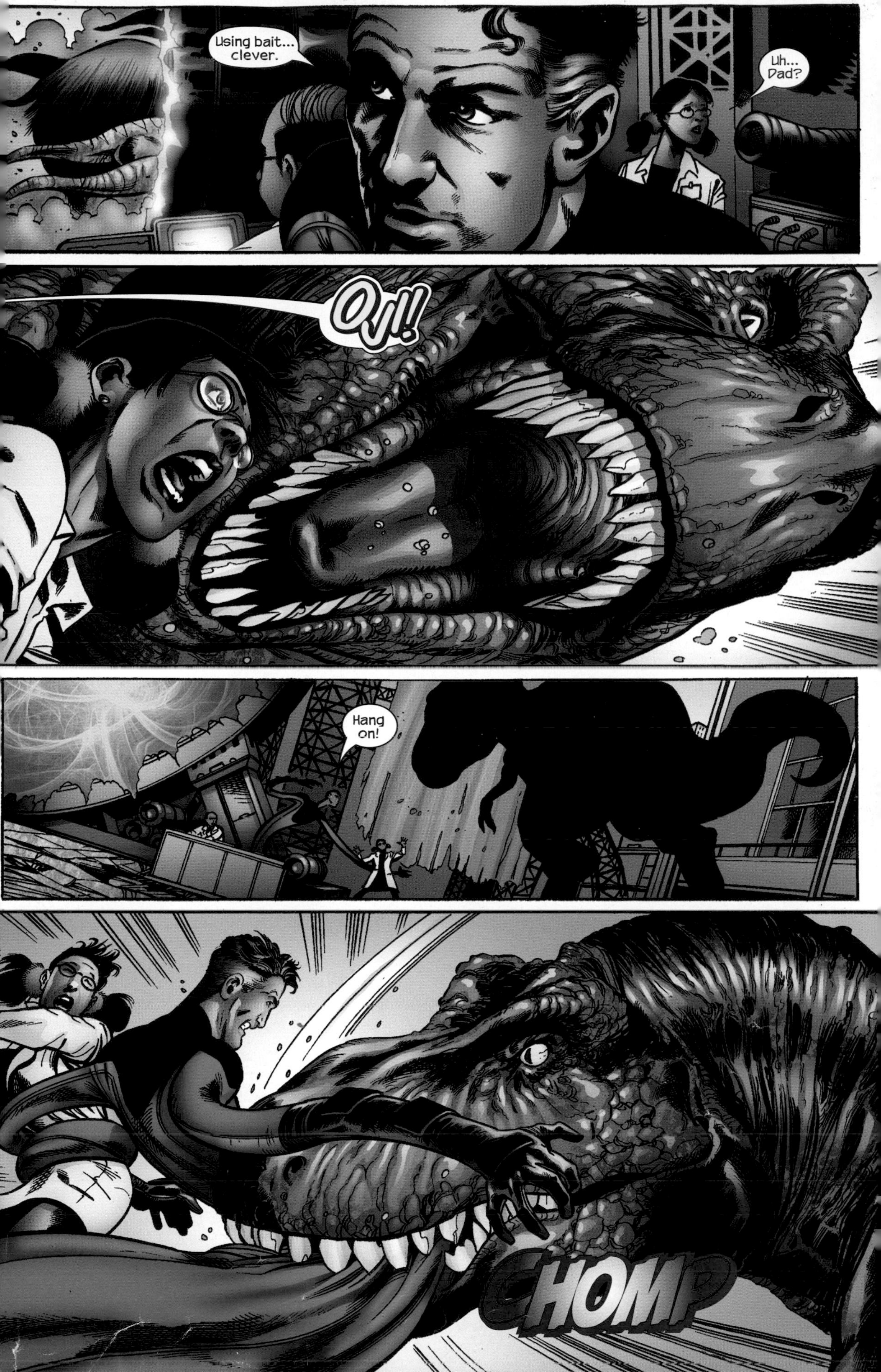
Using bait... clever.
Uh... Dad?
OW!!
Hang on!
CHOMP

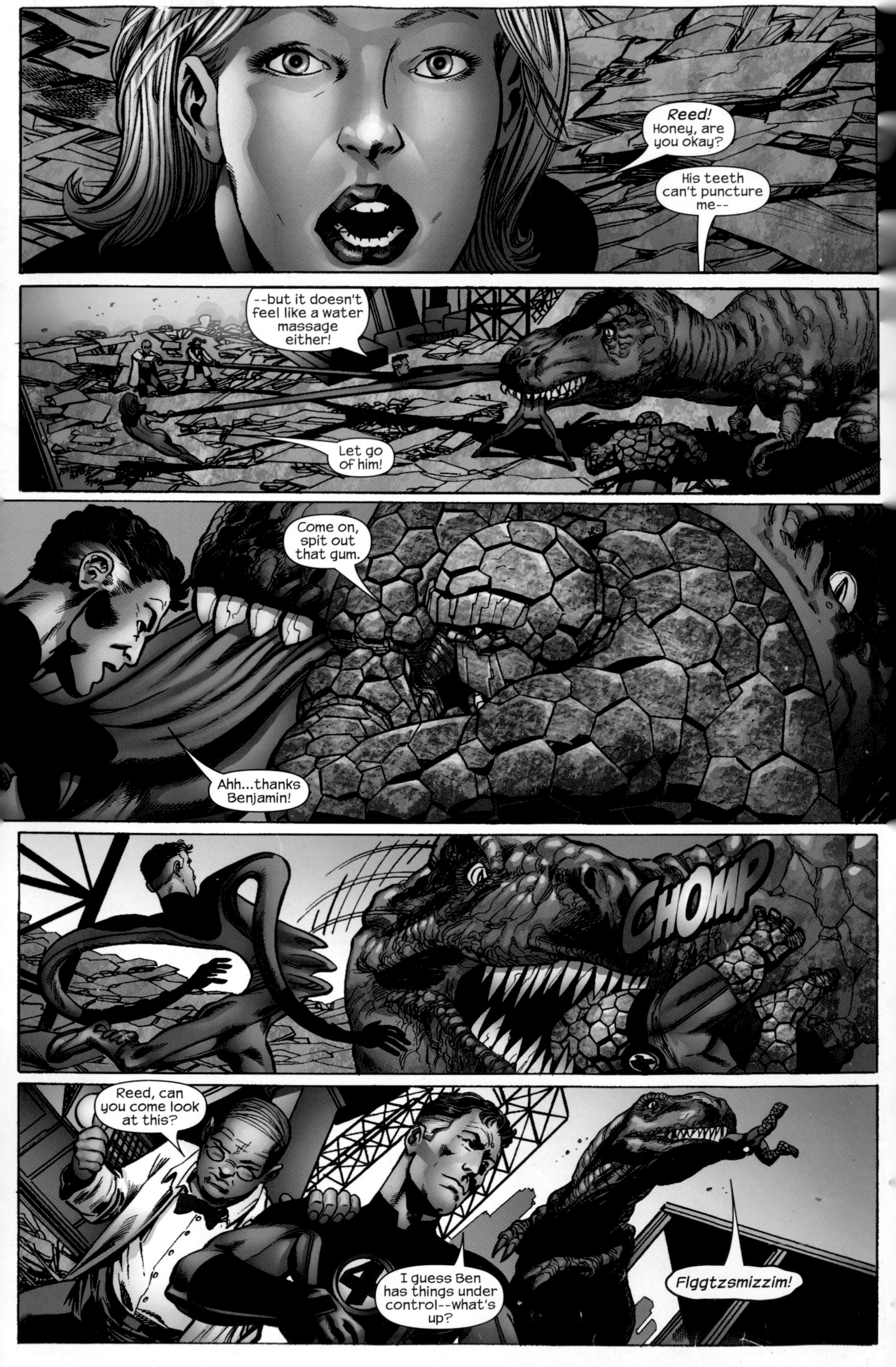
Reed! Honey, are you okay?
His teeth can't puncture me--
--but it doesn't feel like a water massage either!
Let go of him!
Come on, spit out that gum.
Ahh...thanks Benjamin!
CHOMP
Reed, can you come look at this?
I guess Ben has things under control--what's up?
Flggtzsmizzim!

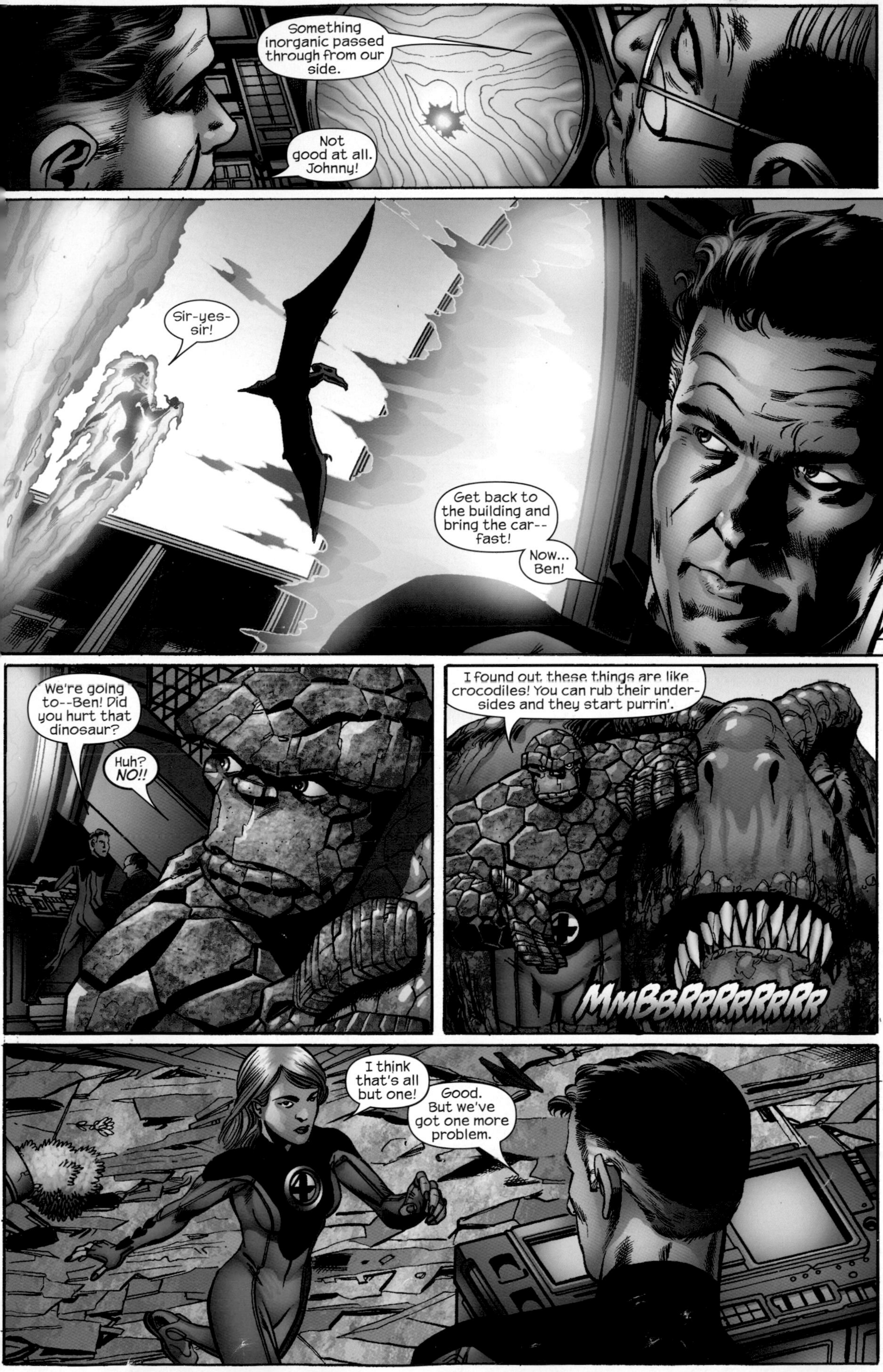
Something inorganic passed through from our side.
Not good at all. Johnny!
Sir-yes-sir!
Get back to the building and bring the car-- fast!
Now... Ben!
We're going to--Ben! Did you hurt that dinosaur?
Huh? NO!!
I found out these things are like crocodiles! You can rub their under-sides and they start purrin'.
MMBBRRRRRRRR
I think that's all but one!
Good. But we've got one more problem.

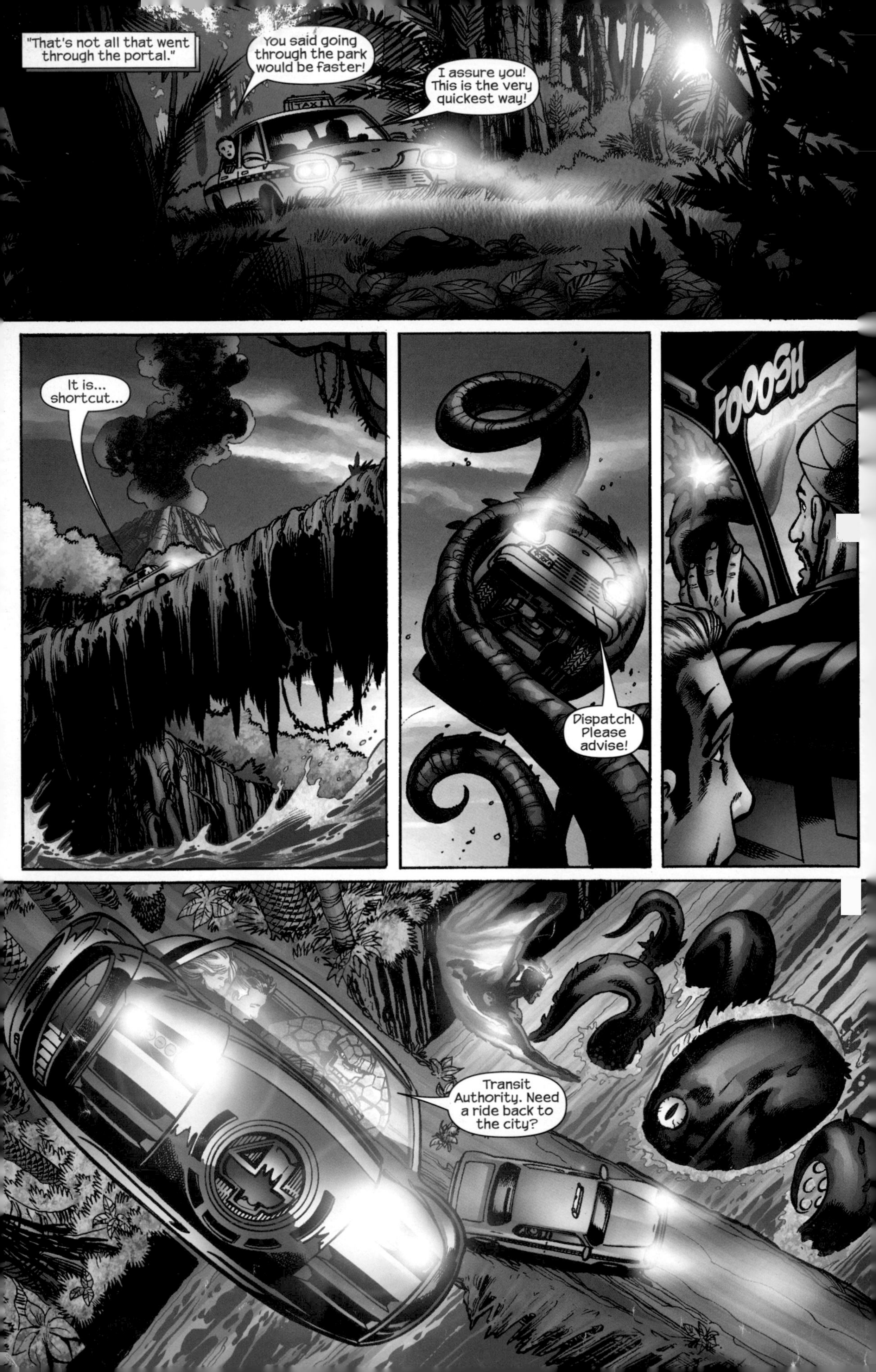
"That's not all that went through the portal."
You said going through the park would be faster!
I assure you! This is the very quickest way!
It is... shortcut...
Dispatch! Please advise!
FOOOSH
Transit Authority. Need a ride back to the city?

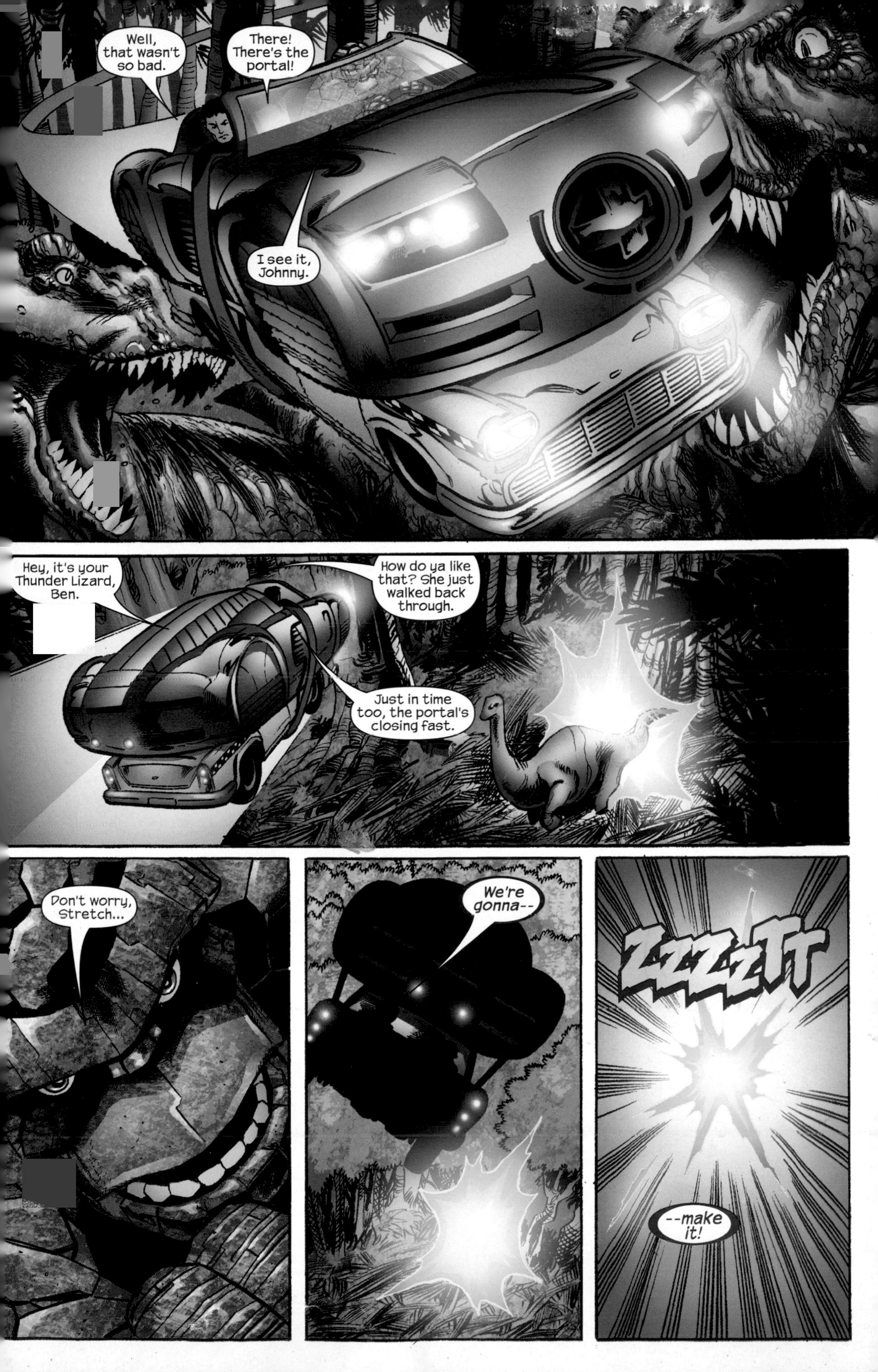
Well, that wasn't so bad.
There! There's the portal!
I see it, Johnny.
Hey, it's your Thunder Lizard, Ben.
How do ya like that? She just walked back through.
Just in time too, the portal's closing fast.
Don't worry, Stretch...
We're gonna--
ZZZZTT
--make it!

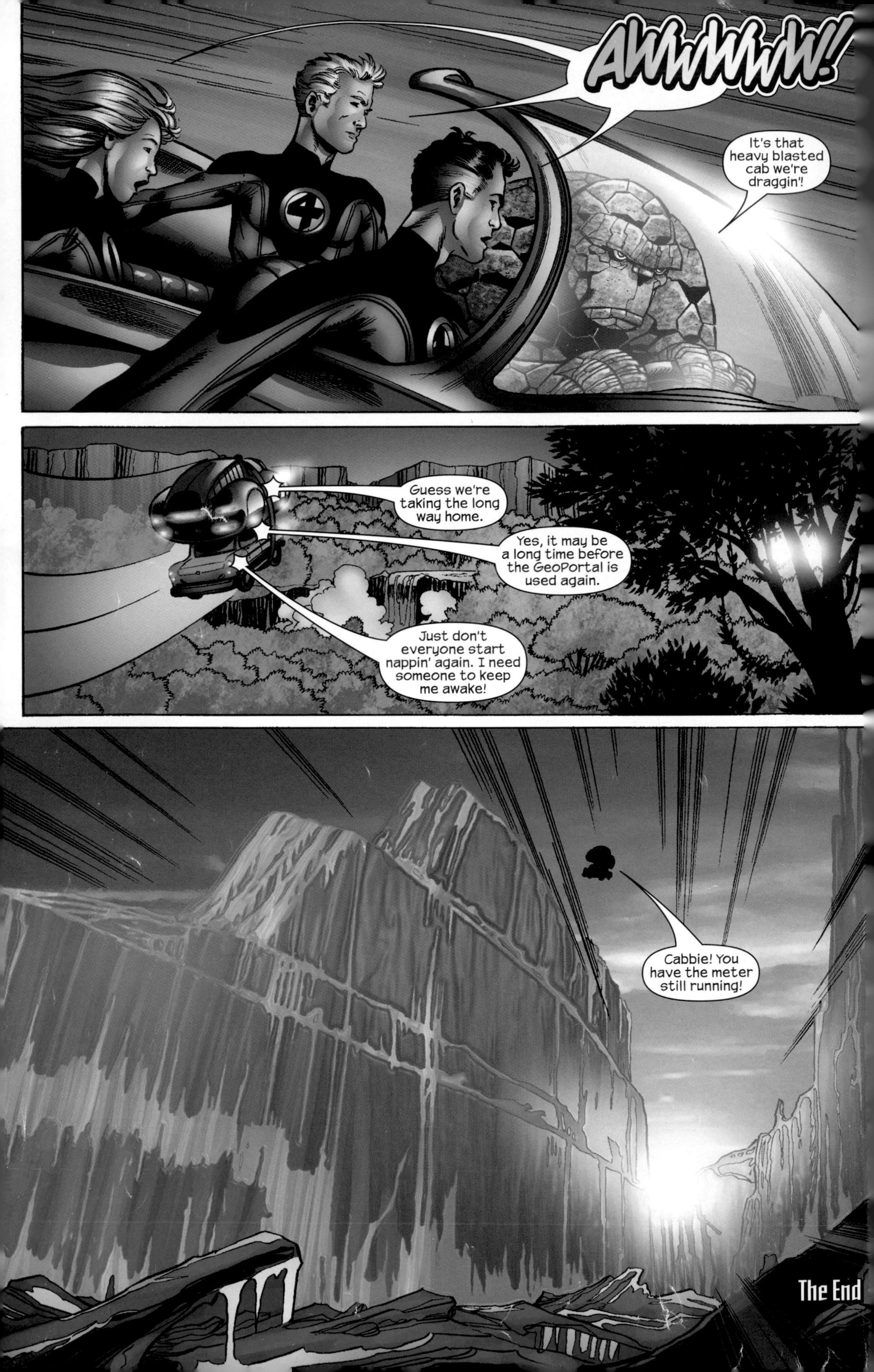
AHHHHHH!
It's that heavy blasted cab we're draggin'!
Guess we're taking the long way home.
Yes, it may be a long time before the GeoPortal is used again.
Just don't everyone start nappin' again. I need someone to keep me awake!
Cabbie! You have the meter still running!
The End